Girl with words–
a little bit sandy...
a little bit breezy...
...and a lot salty

Girl with words–
a little bit sandy...
a little bit breezy...
...and a lot salty

Wendy O'Hanlon
A Poetry Collection

Illustrations by Michelle Mann
www.michellemannart.com

Book layout by Aishah Macgill
www.finitepublishing.com

Cover Photo by Sherrie Terkuile

Categories: Poetry, Fiction.

ISBN 978-0-6455824-1-3

Tawnatelee Publishing House

"This beautiful personal collection of poems, enhanced with gentle monochrome images, is deeply relatable and enriching. Savouring each poem is like dipping into an array of delectable chocolates, some are sweet, some are bitter, but the experience is sublime." Diane Priestley, UK journalist and author

"In her poetry collection, Girl With words, Wendy O'Hanlon's words come from a place of love for her family and a true pride for her community on the Sunshine Coast. Through her array of experiences and creative talents, Wendy's poems speak of many subjects, yet her humour and enthusiasm for life always shines through. A woman with heart!" Gerard Traub, Australian poet and author

I love Wendy's book, I love the journey, the simple and yet profound road trip through a woman's life. I love the world and personal views so plainly and painfully expressed. I love the love story, the devoted daughter, sister and mother, the never pretentious and the always so human feel. I love the you and the me of this book. I love the generous measures of passion and scorn expressed in these pages and I resign to never betray the author for fear of her penning a poem about me." Joe Lynch, Australian/Irish poet & artist

"Wendy O'Hanlon has a wonderfully strong and passionate voice... funny too. My favourites were the two poems about the whales... When the Whale Came and I Can't See the Whales Anymore... were marvellously present and then gone. But I also was moved by many more. Wendy's performance at her books' launch was very special!" Rose Allan, Australian author and editor

Wendy O'Hanlon is a natural-born creative. She has settled into a beautiful, creative space with her first poetry collection, Girl with words. Bravo!" Gail Forrer, Australian journalist and editor

Wendy O'Hanlon's poetry is so original, clever, humorous, insightful and thought provoking. Such a wonderful first collection and I look forward to many more." Jackie B, Australian author

"Dear Wendy, I am just here at Ra Healing Food Café on Gili Air, Indonesia. I got stuck on the island. Leafing through your Girl with words poetry book really filled my heart. Grieve, so much helped me yesterday when closing the year. Endless Possibilities is how I am now – ready to be happy again. Moon and the Sun relates to my relationship on the other side of the world. Thank you for your beautiful and inspiring words." Instagram message from German traveller Nela Knaup (Nelaninx)

Dedication

I dedicate this book, my first poetry anthology, with great love to my folks and youngest brother... my Dad, Bill O'Hanlon; my Mum, Beryl O'Hanlon (nee Menzies); and my youngest brother Daren O'Hanlon. They have passed. They always supported me with love and were proud of me. They taught me that family is everything. I was truly blessed being born into this hard-working, innovative and humble family. And I know I have continued this family strength and love with my amazing young adult sons Billy and Jaye. I'm here because of you.

Thank you.

Foreword

Finally! After a lifetime of writing, here is my first poetry anthology. I've been writing poetry all my life. My beautiful, busy life has now given me the support, space and opportunity in presenting to you the first of many books. I hope you enjoy these poems... some of them spoken-word pieces... some of them just idle thoughts scribbled down quickly while walking the beach. I've chosen pieces from my childhood, teenage, young adult and older adult years.

And huge thanks to so many of you beautiful human beans who have inspired, supported and loved me all these years. It matters. In the final stages of publishing this first anthology, I was struggling with how to arrange the poems in sections. I didn't want to call the sections 'Part One...' or 'In the beginning...' Then my long-time journo friend Trina McLellan nailed it: "girl with words – a little bit sandy, a little bit breezy and a lot salty". And just like that, it all fell in to place!

And remember – poetry is part fiction, part fact and a whole lot of imagination. Enjoy.

Much luv and hugzz,

Wendyoh.

Contents

a little bit sandy... 1

A House – The Eremite 3
A Stranger's Face 5
Blackbird 7
Endless Possibilities...9
Flowers.. 11
Friendship 13
Grieve 15
I can't see the whales anymore........................ 17
I thread my new clothes 19
Moon and the Sun... 21
My Safe Place 23
Old Man 25
Somewhere in the South Pacific 29
Stop the Pollution... 31
Surreal Saturdays 33
Tobacco... 34
When the Whale Came 36
"21 Reasons Why I Love You" 38

a little bit breezy........................... 41

All Men Are Bastards 43
Are We Really Wishing.................................... 46
Our Lives Away? 46
Elephant 48
He 51
I Lost It 53
Laugh 55
This.. 57

I am...59

Lost..60

Monsters 62

Old Love...65

Poetry 67

The Fly 68

Touching..71

Travel...73

Two Wheels...74

You have to pick your own war........................77

You've Robbed Me 79

...and a lot salty..........................81

An Anti-Valentine's Day Poem
(for all you lovers out there)............................83

Couch 85

Elastic Band..87

I am not a Number..89

I Draw Circles 91

I thought you were my rock 93

Never Betray a Writer 94

Paris – an anti-love poem 96

Pockets 99

Prejudice 100

Viva La Revolution! 102

Wendy O'Hanlon..104

Illustrator Michelle Mann...............................106

Hi... from girlwithwords 108

Create your own poetry 110

Start your own poetry or
spoken word group/event 112

a
little
bit
sandy...

Photo ©Pearse O'Halloran, Unsplash

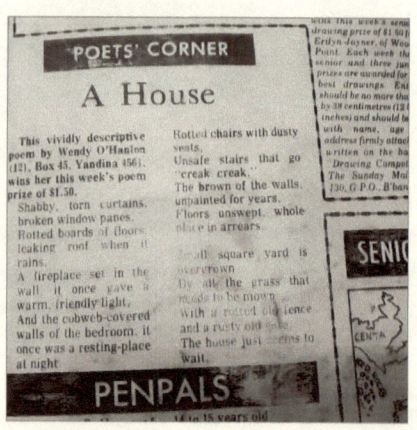

This is my first-ever published poem. I was 12 years old when 'The House – The Eremite' was published in the Queensland Schools quarterly magazine and I was in Year 7 at Maroochy River State Primary School. The school inspector had visited our little, one-teacher school and read my poem. He asked me what an 'eremite' was and asked if he could publish it in the schools' magazine.

Later that year, December 2, 1973, my poem appeared in The Sunday Mail's Poetry Corner as I had won their weekly poetry prize and the princely sum of $1.50. You may notice that the 5th verse of the poem, where the eremite enters the story, was cut to fit to space – as was the title. I was still a very excited girl!

Publication Date Of my first poem.

A House – The Eremite

Shabby, torn curtains,
Broken window panes.
Rotted boards of floors,
Leaking roof when it rains.

A fireplace set in the wall,
It once gave a warm, friendly light.
And the cobweb-covered walls of the bedroom,
It once was a resting place at night.

Rotted chairs with dusty seats,
Unsafe stairs that go "creak, creak".
The brown of the walls unpainted for years,
Floors unswept, whole place in arrears.

An eremite once took refuge there,
Sore was he,
When he could not bear,
The cold, rough winds that rushed everywheres,
Through doorways, windows and under the stairs.

Small, square yard is overgrown,
By all the grass that needs to be mown.
With a rotted old fence and a rusty old gate,
The house just seems to wait.

©Wendy O'Hanlon aged 12, 1973

A Stranger's Face

You're like sand thru my fingers,
Early morning fog
Across a wasteland,
Smoke and mirrors,
A stranger's face.

©Wendy O'Hanlon August, 2019

This poem is about the Kanakas who were brought from their Solomon Island/Fiji and Pacific Island homelands to work on Queensland cane farms in the 1900s — indentured and virtually enslaved.

Blackbird

Early in the morning you sing your song
In a sweet voice filled with woe.
Telling of your life and how it's gone wrong
Blackbird caught in a web of snow.

Your days are filled with wasted dreams,
You have no place to go.
There's no meaning left in life it seems.
Blackbird caught in a web of snow.

Gone is your land of forest and brush,
In their stead are struggling canes laid in long, straight rows.
Gone is your nest, lay safe amongst the thrush,
Now sleep is hard when the cold wind blows.

Though your plumage
Is as black as a moonless night,
Within your soul the warmth glows,
And the lights in your eyes are kind.
Unlike those who give the cage
Their souls are so cold and so white,
Dead are their eyes
Because to love they are blind.

You work right through the heat of the day
As the sunlight paints your sweat 'till it glows.
Spread your wings and fly to freedom,
Alas, there is no way.
Blackbird born in a web of snow.

Photo ©-Vvelizar Ivanov, Unsplash

Endless Possibilities

I want to laugh
And dance again
I want to be surprised
I want to trust again
I want to relish plans
For the future
I want to love again…
To tingle again.

The world has opened up
Endless possibilities
The excitement of
The known
And unknown.

I'm ready
I'm propelling forward
With a sure grip
On a life force
I have rediscovered
And claimed
As my own.

©Wendy O'Hanlon, September, 2019

Flowers

Oh God, when I die
I hope there aren't cameras!
I hope my life doesn't demand
Cameras at my funeral.

I hope I'm not resurrected
Every decade
And celebrated posthumously.

I hope my casket isn't flashed
Around the world
In living rooms
And bars.

I hope my grieving people
Aren't wide-angled,
Zoomed in to, still shot
And rolled off the presses.

I hope newsrooms around the world
Don't reach for
My obit file to add a final date.

Oh God, when I die, I hope there aren't cameras!
I hope I'm not that accessible, that public.

Oh God, when I die
Don't bring the world to me
Or me to the world.

Just leave me be.
Don't build a monolith.
Just leave me flowers.

©Wendy O'Hanlon, 1986

Friendship

A giggle of girls
A laughter of ladies
A chatter of chicks.

Sun, surf, sand, salty sweat,
Hugs and tears
Is what friendship
Is about
Through all these years.
Friday frolics forever!

©Wendy O'Hanlon, September, 2019

Photo ©Geran De Klerk, Unsplash

Grieve

Grieve madly
Sadly
Proudly
Like an elephant.

Roar the eulogy
Pound your fists in to the sand.

Scream at the sky
Fall down
Cry mountains
Feel invisible hugs.

Grieve loud and long
Silently and in moments.

Grieve.

*Written after the death in August of that year of my dear friend of
more than 30 years and former father-in-law, Poppa Clive.*

I can't see the whales anymore

I sit on my son's verandah
And watch the ocean disappear
Brick by brick
Month after month
Until I can only look up
At the sky…
Sigh…
And imagine the whales passing by.

©Wendy O'Hanlon, October 14, 2019

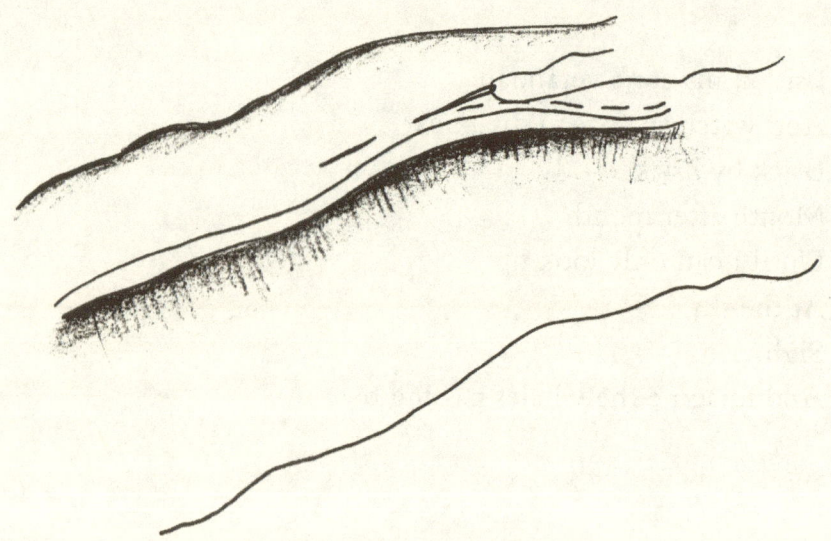

I thread my new clothes

So I thread my new clothes
From fabrics all a–glitter
Comfortably worn and repurposed.

©Wendy O'Hanlon, January 1, 2019

Moon and the Sun

If I was the moon
And you were the sun
We'd catch glimpses of each other
Before the day was done...

We'd whisper of our journeys
Around the curvature of this Earth

And when I'm waning,
A shadow of myself,
You'd rise brightly
And shine
Above the clouds.

If I was the moon
And you were the sun
We'd dance across the skies
Forever.

©Wendy O'Hanlon, September, 2019

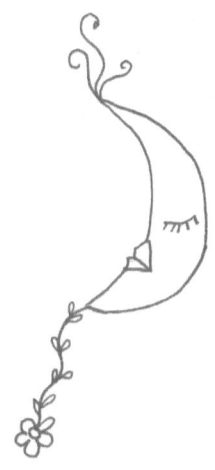

My Safe Place

You were my safe place
That is why it hurts
So much
Why I am so broken.

I'll pretend you are working away
In a god-forsaken dusty red dot
On the map
In the desert
In a donger.

We are working hard to buy
A farm
Filled with gardens to eat.
Cats, dogs, pigs and llamas
To feed.

But I know…
I know.

I need to find
Another anchor.
Maybe it's me…
All along…
All alone.

©Wendy O'Hanlon, July, 2019

Photo ©*Bruno Martins, Unsplash*

Old Man

Hey, Old Man
Yes, you on the bench
I've been watching you
and wondering.

Where do you come from, old man
Where have you been.
What is it that you have to say
That will never be told.

Your life, was it a hard one?
Was it tough?

Do you remember with bitterness
Your young blurry days
Or are they that bright light
you keep searching for?

Did you go to war, old man
Or did you stay home to taunts?
Did the hard times affect you
Or were you well padded?

Did you have parents for long
A good family life
Or were you a drifter,
An unsettled sole.

Did you do good, old man
Do you remember lots
Or were you evil,
They'll remember you too.

Continued overleaf

As you sit where you sit
Quite peaceful it seems
What goes thru your mind
What goes thru your dreams?

Are you happy, old man
At peace with your lot
Are you bitter and torn
And tied like a knot.

Who waits for you old man
a wife, generations
or are you alone
save your own contemplations.

I wonder, old man
about you
about all of you.

What in the world
Do your old frames tell me
Why do I feel you are all history walking
What is it about
A lifetime on two feet
Decades remembered, cocooned in your hair.

Was it worth it,
Is it still

Continued next page

Please tell me, tell me
But a quick summary, mind you
Not day by day
My life's still young
And its slipping away

Tell me all
But tell me quick
I'll have plenty of time later
When I have to carry the stick.

So tell me now
While I'm still young
I can spare an hour
So quicken your tongue

I've a hundred questions
maybe more
So a quick little chat
And I'll head for the door,

There's still more you say?
Oh, well, must run.
I'll make it another day
It has been fun.

See ya later…

Old Man!

WHERE HAVE YOU GONE!

©*Wendy O'Hanlon, 1976*   *Written for a major Year 11 English project.*

Somewhere in the South Pacific

We've done things
You and Me
The amount of times we counted our dollars
Frowned, then laughed
And had a happy spree.

The amount of times we've gone around in circles
Surfaced, gone under again,
Then come up for air.

But we've done that
We've been there
It was all fun, worry and tears.

Now we're somewhere in the South Pacific.
Who really cares?
Just You and Me.

©Wendy O'Hanlon, 1986

Stop the Pollution

Stop the pollution
Where's the solution?
Why must we ruin
Our pure fresh air?
Does anybody really care?
About stopping
The dropping
Everywhere!

© Wendy O'Hanlon, aged 11, 1972

Note: My first public poetry performance, apart from our little school recitals in front of a total student population of between 8 and 15 kids – depending on cane season. Performed in front of a large church congregation at the age of 11

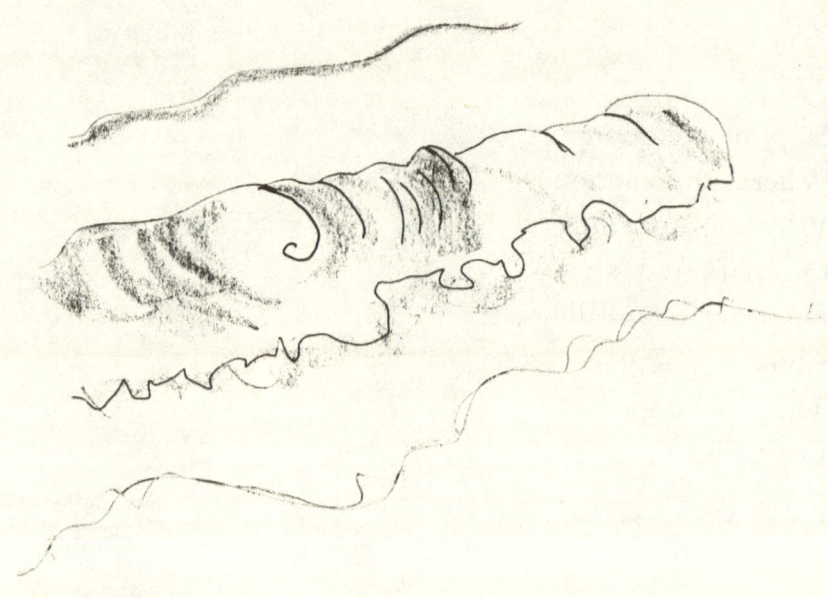

Surreal Saturdays

Salutations Saturday!
Salty shiny shimmery Saturday
Slipping through my slimy seaweedy fingers
Rub with sand! Superb.
Soon sultry Sunday will
Slip over the scarlet horizon.
Success! Made it through another
Seemingly scattered week… again!

©Wendy O'Hanlon, 1986

Tobacco

Back then,

When there was no internet or Google,
It was an adventure, a secret trial,
'being naughty', 'being grown-up'.
Two kids growing up on a cane farm,
Wild tobacco plants growing randomly and freely.
Our parents neither drank nor smoked –
this was our secret pact.
Legs dangling over the riverbank,
toes kissing the water,
we opened our secret stash
of dried tobacco leaves,
old newspaper and matches.
We would master this thing called 'smoking'.
Coughing. Burnt fingers from the newspaper burning
quicker than the leaves. A slight 'spin'. More coughing.
'Really?' This is not fun. Smoking is not the thrill we
expected. Adults are nuts!'

Flash forward:

Young adults, moved out of home, freedom, wages.
'A packet of red Winnies, please.' And we are allowed.
We've joined the adult world of kegs of beer and Winnies
and Camel and Marlborough and Alpine.

Continued next page

Flash forward:

'Smoking during pregnancy is not advised'.

Flash forward:
Years of abstinence fall away. A nagging cough. Expensive hypnotherapy sessions, $1 a ciggie, Rollies don't give that buzz. I need petro chemicals, tyre rubber and all manner of nasties thrown in to the mix to satisfy my lungs and my cravings.

I crave abstinence. I want to embrace it so hard that the smoke and tar spew from my lungs.
Abstinence, be my friend.

©Wendy O'Hanlon, 2018

When the Whale Came

When the whale came
800 hearts and souls
Forgot their earthly struggle,
Forgot their bills and worries,
squabbles with family
and promises to friends.

When the whale beached,
Floundering, gasping for air,
The people came
from north, south and west
Like they were tuned to a sonar signal
To meet at a small point
On a long beach
Where one big, black barnacled creature
from the deep
was no longer in the deep
but sinking into the sands
unable to turn back.

Continued next page

When the whale left
800 hearts and souls
Cried for joy
Hearts doing backflips
Hugging strangers.

It didn't take that long, though,
For the euphoria to fade...
And all the worries and squabbles
and struggles start shrouding their lives again.

But every now and then
they tell their story of when the whale came
And a bit of sunshine cracks into their human shells.

©*Wendy O'Hanlon, October, 1996*

Photo ©Todd Craven, Unsplash

"21 Reasons Why I Love You"

Number One: My sons

Born of Celtic and Viking stock, you are mighty human beans! Tall, strong, happy, smart, quick-witted, funny, individual, confident, big-hearted...

You are the best mates anyone could have... and have given more than the shirts off your backs to help out a friend so many times. And, YES, you do respect women. And for that I love you most. You both care about justice and fairness. You are Global Citizens. You have traveled the world so many times in your lives... starting as babies. You respect all GOOD people in the world... no matter their skin tone or language.

The best sons this wistful cane-farmers' daughter could ever have dreamed up!

Billy and Jaye, you have both found a focus and direction and claimed it! I'm a Happy, Happy Mum, because you are both Happy Young Men.

Continued next page

Number 2: My friends

Yes, yes, yes! I am never on time. Sometimes I'm dippy, always striving too high, falling fast and up again, just as quickly.

It's those hugs, baby! They are the best. And crying and laughing at the same time, without alcohol, just a morning beach walk and a brunch latte? Priceless!

You are all different, beautiful, clever, funny, quirky, loving, down-to-earth... some, we grew up together as cane-farmers' kids on Dunethin Rock Road, Maroochy River. Some, we have seen our children grow from possums to persons, and some, my beautiful friends I have met since... our jigsaw works but there is always room for a new piece in this puzzle. A bigger, beautiful picture, forever being painted... in watercolour, sand, pastels, oil... that photo in our minds.

More hugs?

Collectively, my sons, my friends... you define ME. You call me out, you pick me up, without you all, I would not be this Wendy. Thank you all.

21 Reasons Why I Love You...

But who's counting?

©Wendy O'Hanlon, October, 1996

a
little
bit
breezy...

Photo ©Tyler Nix, Unsplash

All Men Are Bastards

All men are bastards,
With their raging testosterone levels
They start wars,
They make whores
And without them we women could have
Our boobs and our jowls hanging down to the floors
No more nipping and tucking
Primping and plucking.
Bastards!

All men are bastards
What they consider their one act of unselfish love
Ends up, nine months later
With the woman enduring nothing short of torture – labour!
Torn in half
Spine cracking
Only to deliver another
Butt-smacking… male
Of the species!
Bastards!

Ask any woman – on the street, in the house, on the stage
And they will reply with such pent-up rage
All men are bastards!

Oh, except for my father
And my two brothers and sons
I see no reason as to why
The male race was begun.

Continued overleaf

Women are kind, caring, nurturing souls
Who care not a fig for powerful roles
Instead to live quietly, happy and free.
Free of wars, free of hatred, free of greed.

For the male of the species
Has so little progressed
From the dark Neanderthal cave
And the beating on chests
To assert their dominion,
To pillage and conquer
All in the name of family honour.

So in this 21st Century
Of internets and webs,
The global economy
And test-tube sex instead,
I ask you, if all men are bastards
And women superior,
Why must society remain inferior?
Lose the men, the bastards,
Genetically wipe them out!
We women don't need them,
Without a doubt.

All men are bastards,
They curse and sweat about
Their bread-winning role
The man of the manor
The burden they carry.

Continued next page

Yet, they run… from dirty nappies, children's fights,
Wives crying, housework… all the little things in life
That are, in fact, life.

They bemoan their status
With elbows on a bar
With mates who don't emote
They talk of business, the next car.
Arrive home with a nudge to
The day-weary wife
And expect the best night of sex
They may get in their life!
Bastards!

All men are bastards – Bastards!
I'll say it again,
All men are bastards
And I only hope that my two sons
Grow up to be happy, healthy, well-adjusted
Women!

©Wendy O'Hanlon, 2002

I was inspired to write this poem when invited to speak at a Maroochydore Rotary Club dinner by the late Maroochy Shire councillor Arnie Barnes. There was a bit of a kerfuffle about women joining a particular chapter of this group. I worked with the Sunshine Coast Daily newspaper at the time as a journalist but never covered this story. So, when Arnie (a funny bloke and a good man) asked me to speak at his Rotary club's monthly dinner, I was happy to and thought I'd talk about working with the media. Arnie interrupted me in the first minute. "Wendy, didn't you read the program? Your topic is 'All Men are Bastards'." It was a joke, but I delivered my media spiel and promised them I would address that topic the next meeting. I did. They loved it and sent it to their national Rotary magazine!

Are We Really Wishing Our Lives Away?

Are we really wishing our lives away?
Are we all just waiting for something to happen…
I can't wait till…
I can't wait till Tuesday
When my friend comes around with his music
I can't wait till that band is on – till I get paid.

Are you sitting in an office somewhere – getting here-and-
now fleeting glimpses of the world out there?
Do you look up and realise its rained – half an hour ago or
more.

So you're not in an office, you're at home
There's no work for you at all
So, what are you wishing away?
What is it that you can't wait for?
A job, perhaps?

Continued next page

Are you sure this is your dream?
Who do you want to be?
What are you waiting for?

Or have you given up
Now all you want is some peace in your mind
Or just blot your mind out instead.
Who do you want to be?
What are you waiting for?
Do you wake up sometimes screaming:
What, where, why, help me!
Or does that happen anytime, awake at home, talking,
Just acting the day thru?

It would be nice wouldn't it?
To stop wishing, I mean.

©Wendy O'Hanlon, 1986

Elephant

The elephant in the room…
I can see him
He's always there politely sitting in the corner
Cross-legged
Comfortable
Not threatening
Sometimes quietly snoozing…
Just there.

Sometimes I wave
And I swear his little tail waves back!
He blinks: "Guess my name."
But I won't play that game.

He has his silent job.
I look up at him sometimes
I can see him, you know.
But I mostly ignore him…
And he's okay with that.

Continued next page

Sometimes we have brief eye contact
But I look away quickly
I really just don't wanna know, you know?
I like my cocoon
It's safe here.
In Winter.
In Lockdown.

When the world becomes "real" again,
My elephant 'buddy'
Will move to
Another corner
Of another room.

I know he isn't real.
But I did see him.

©Wendy O'Hanlon, June 6, 2020

He

He's my madness
He's my comfort zone
He keeps me at arm's length
He holds me tight through the night.

He makes me want to scream inside
He makes me want to laugh out loud.

He's my lockdown lover
He's my friend.

When will this bubble
Ever end?

©Wendy O'Hanlon, August 15, 2020

Photo ©Marek Piwnicki, Unsplash

I Lost It

A spoken word came
In to my head
Then a line, a verse, more words… a poem.

I raced to find pen and paper
Sat down
And started to recall, retain this gift.

But I lost it
That first word, the opening line, the ending.

Just like that it had been snatched away
Carried on the wind
To find another
dreamy writer's mind.

©Wendy O'Hanlon, September 2019

Laugh

Laugh
Go on
Stretch that face
Crinkle it good.
Laugh
Why not?
      Ha

            Ha.

This

This is cynical stuff
Watch what you say.
They're listening
They do every day.

©Wendy O'Hanlon, 1986

I am

I'm at an all-time high
I must be a statistic
I must be the rate of murder
I must be the rate of robberies
I must be the rate of prejudice
I must be the rate of shit.
Yeah, I'm at an all-time high
Life's really great
Just don't tell me about it.

©Wendy O'Hanlon, 1986

Lost

Sometimes…
In my dreams
I am lost.
I'm walking along cobblestone streets
With bare feet
Because I've lost my shoes
Running from a tavern 'cavern'
Trying to catch up with friends
Because I'd been animatedly talking
To strangers… again.

Sometimes I am lost
At a big village music festival
Sloshing through the mud
In bare feet
Because I've lost my thongs
One at a time
Suctioned by the slime
Looking for that new young duo
With the rave reviews
Playing in the open-mic tent.

Continued next page

Google says these dreams mean
'a sign of anxiety...
Feeling like you are losing the ground
Beneath your feet'.

Sometimes...
In these dreams
I have also lost my bag with phone and purse
And so have to keep walking
To find where I started from.

Sometimes...
In these dreams
I do retrace my steps
And find my bag, my friends and home base.

Sometimes I wake up before the end,
Get out of bed,
Make a cup of coffee
To shake the dream
Out of my head,
And then slowly drift back to sleep
Only to start all over again.

©Wendy O'Hanlon, April, 2022

Monsters

My friend,
He sees monsters.
Sadly, they look like you or me.
Any age, any gender,
Any ethnicity.

The monsters, they stalk solo
Or in packs of two or three.

They loom and prowl at libraries,
Fish n chips shops,
In parks or along the beach.

They track his car,
Whisper together,
Text message to stay within reach.

These monsters, though, are in his head
And attack with frightening speed.
Many times these monsters
have actually scared me.

Continued next page

It's tragic that such a beautiful mind and soul,
Can be devoured whole
By monsters
Who were invited in
When he was young and shy
And trying to fit in.
That long-ago addiction
To heroin
Has left damaging track marks
In his psyche.

I pray the monsters
will discard this prey
This shining soul
Who is fading away.

Yes, I have a friend who sees monsters
Every day.
And every day I fail
To chase those monsters away.

©Wendy O'Hanlon, April, 2022

Old Love

No-one is ever going
To love this face
My face
As much as you did

Old hands clasping
Forever lasting
But this is not
The story
For
You
And
Me

I'll see you
On the other
Side
One day…

©Wendy O'Hanlon, July, 2019

Poetry

It doesn't need to be all rat–a–tat–tat
It could spring from your mind, just like that
It could be emotional and soft
with rhyming and timing
Or it could burst through your ears
Like a firework.

You can stamp and rage and shake your fist
Poetry is all of this.

Writing poetry clears you
Performing those words, frees you
Even if you think you can't write a word
Poetry is the platform
For your feelings to be heard.

©Wendy O'Hanlon, 2018

The Fly

I saw a fly
passing by.
It flew, it flew
and it flew by.

I wonder why
that particular fly
caught my eye
as it did you.

The fly, I cry
has long passed by
But yet speaks about
it's mean feat
of passing by
while we watch.

Despite all our schemes
To kill the fly
This fly
Has long passed by.

Continued next page

But while we
plot
and plan,
The fly,
that very same fly
passes by again.
And what have we learnt?

That flies
aren't worth a single line
an ounce of time
of rhetoric
or rhyme.

Still. Long fly the fly that twice flew by.
He flew, he flies,
He is, he does, a fly.

©Wendy O'Hanlon, 1986

*Also published as a colour children's book called
'The Fly' illustrated by Michelle Mann.*

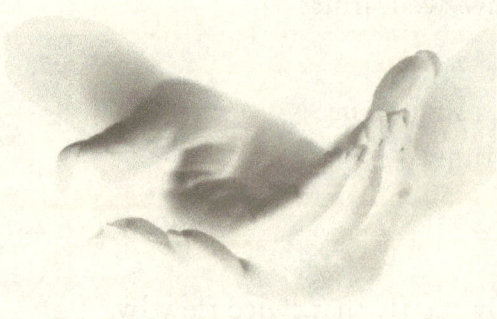

Touching

The day that touching was banned
I looked at my hand
And,
Held it in my other
… and
Squeezed.

©Wendy O'Hanlon, March, 2020

Written at the very start of Covid lockdowns in Queensland, Australia.

Travel

I travel through your veins
Like heroin.

I travel through your ears
Like a Hurricane jet over The Bays.

I travel through your eyes
Like an Aurora Borealis.

I travel through your spine
Like a crack of thunder.

I travel through your toes
Like cliff-top perch adrenalin.

I travel through your nose
Like a tickling feather.

Take my hand and travel with me
To Antarctica, Iceland, Africa and Tonga.

Let me travel within you
And you within me
We have our passports.
Let's go!

©Wendy O'Hanlon, 2018

Two Wheels

The wind,
Like a thousand
Winged needles
Piercing my face.
Two wheels and
I'm free.

"You waste your life riding around
 With your mates in a pack.
You're no better than the dirt on the ground
That you mark with your tyre track."

No longer
Have I legs,
Man and machine
Born in to one,
Now complete,
I am alive

"Late at night around the street,
In a black leather jacket, concealed in the sleeve,
Are the knives and chains you use on those you meet.
With breaking store window and the rev of the bike, you leave."

Continued next page

I care not
What the people think,
They don't know life...

I ask for nothing
But to be free from slander.

For
My life
Is real.

For
My life
Is two wheels.

©Wendy O'Hanlon, 1976

Written for a major Year 11 English project.

You have to pick your own war

I want to save:
Orang-utans, sun bears, lions, koalas, wombats…
I want to save:
The Great Barrier Reef, the Murray River, Yaroomba…
I want to save:
Refugees…

I want to save:
Street dogs from a dinner menu…
I want to save:
Venice and The Amazon…

You have to pick your own war…
But first
I have to
Save:
Myself.

©Wendy O'Hanlon, August 13, 2020

Photo ©James Wheeler, Unsplash

You've Robbed Me

You've robbed me of…
Campfire nights
Fish n chips with the crows
Beach walks
A best friend
Happiness
Plans
Holidays
Poetry, music
A safe place, and,
Holding hands
When we are old.

©Wendy O'Hanlon, July, 2019

...and
a
lot
salty

Photo ©Kaja Reichardt, Unsplash

An Anti-Valentine's Day Poem
(for all you lovers out there)

Thanks for the flowers, you cheating bastard, and thanks for the wine, although it's she who likes red, I prefer a bottle of rose instead. Please remember that next time.

And thanks for the Glasgow Kiss, with heavy make-up I can just about get away with this.

And thanks for the extravagant seafood smorgasbord, the salads were divine but I'm allergic to shellfish, perhaps you have forgotten this?

And thanks for the beautiful Valentine's Day card, but my nickname is not 'Blossom', maybe that's your new endearment for me.

And cheers to all our years together, those achingly endless years.

©Wendy O'Hanlon, Valentine's Day, 2019

Written for our regular Words@play spoken-word, open-mic events at Foxys on Coolum.
That event's particular theme was Valentine's Day, so I took the opposite tack.

Couch

I am not your couch
I am not your comfortable landing
I am not a sponge
For you
To expunge
All your troubles and fears
While my life
My existence
Falls on deaf ears.

I am flesh
And bone
And heart
And soul
Not an inanimate object.

I am not your couch
If you want furniture
Try some other
Fool.

©Wendy O'Hanlon, 2022

Elastic Band

On my wrist
I write numbers
In the morning.

These are the number of days
We have not messaged
Spoken
Or seen each other.

As the number increases
I am getting better
And the ink-stained shadows
Beneath the new numbers
Fade.

©Wendy O'Hanlon, July 10, 2019

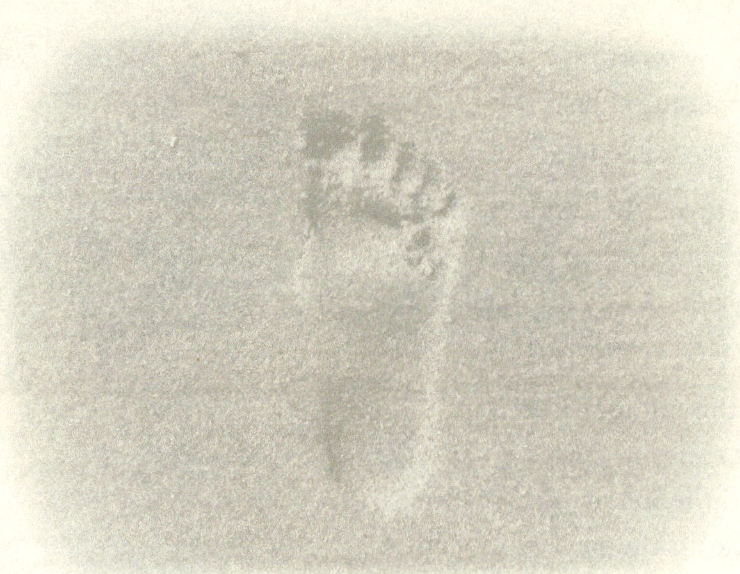

I am not a Number

I am not a number.
I am not my age, my bank balance, my height, my weight.

Zeroes be damned!

I am not a number!

You cannot define me and I will not define myself... by a number.

I am flesh, I am spirit
I am thoughts and sounds.
I am music in waves.

I am.
I am me.
A one-off... Never to be – before or again.

This is my footprint.

I am here.
I cry, I bleed, I laugh, I breathe, I grow, I play, I sing.

I know...
I am....
Me.

©Wendy O'Hanlon, January, 2010

Photo ©Nadine Shaabana, Unsplash

I Draw Circles

I draw circles on you at night
when you are sleeping…
Across your back
with my fingertip
when you are sleeping.

I draw circles across your forehead
at night
with my fingertip
when you are sleeping.

I draw circles around your nipple
at night
with my fingertip
when you are sleeping.

Then I curl my hand in yours
and sleep.

©Wendy O'Hanlon, April, 2020

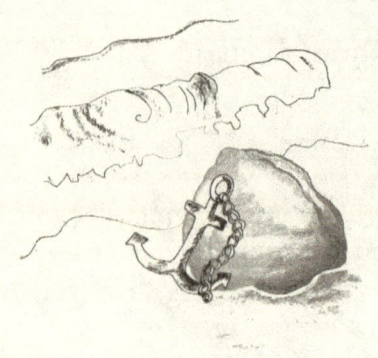

I thought you were my rock

I thought you were my rock, my anchor
But in truth you weighed me down.

I thought you were my left sock
But I was barefoot in the sand all along.

I thought you were my soft, safe place
But you were really
Quicksand.

©Wendy O'Hanlon, May, 2019

Never Betray a Writer

Never betray a writer
Because they'll scrawl on walls
Real and virtual:
"Liar, slyer!"

They'll scream – a guttural scream –
To the heavens
Searing the clouds
Like a laser beam.
Their tears etched in sand and shells.

Never betray a writer
Their pain and heartache
Will be lived again and again
In poems and songs.

Continued next page

Never betray a writer.
They vent their emotions
In words…
the only way they know how to
express…
until they are spent,
hollow,
no longer able to pick up the pen
for fear of releasing
that unfamiliar and unwelcome anger again.

Never betray a writer
Because words are their tools
And their weapons.

Never betray a writer
Because their story
Will be told.

©Wendy O'Hanlon, July, 2019

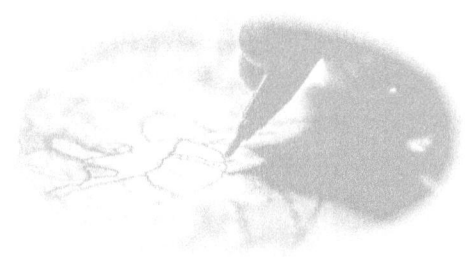

Paris – an anti-love poem

Oh Paris! A cultural burst!!
The Eiffel Tower, the Louvre, the Arc de Triompe
The wide and welcoming Champs-Elysees
Named as a tribute to the Elysian Fields – the mythical
paradise where all dead Greek heroes go.

I remember walking aimlessly under the streetlight glow
Of the Champs-Elysees one chilly night,
The beautiful light rain disguising the tears
Running haphazardly down my face
As the ruddy bruise kept swelling across my left cheek.

Oh, Paris!
The artists, the flair, the fashion, the colours, the chic!
Your many bridges over the River Seine,
Those quaint pedestrian bridges,
The artists plying their craft
with easels at the ready, propped along the pretty river
balustrades.
That little bridge Le Pont Dubilly,
That's where I saw my very first stars.
Oh, not the bright, twinkly kind you find in clear night skies,
The cartoon-character type of stars that circle
around and around your head – think Road Runner and
Coyote.
Halfway across this pretty bridge
My head hit the concrete with just one punch.
Slowly opening my eyes – I saw stars.

Continued next page

Oh, Paris!
The smells of café society, croissants and sweet cakes,
The coffee – oh, the coffee –
The cigarettes and smoking lazily in perfectly proper ashtrays.
Time slows amidst the gorgeous bustle
As these treats are savoured by all the senses.
The glare of his eyes, the intense burning sensation
As he stabs his cigarette in to my outstretched, non-violent palm.

Oh, Paris!
The terror, the bombings, poor Charlie Hebdo.
Oh, Paris.
Why are you shooting writers armed with only their pens?
The City of Love where words are dangerous.
Oh, Paris.
We can taste the hate breeding in your residences.
We breathe the fear lurking along your cobblestone avenues.
Oh, Paris!
I don't love you anymore.

©Wendy O'Hanlon, April, 2018

Pockets

Check your pockets.
Do it again.
Go on. Check your pockets.
I'm not there am I?
Hmm. Cause a friend isn't someone
You keep in your pocket
And pull out whenever
You feel the need.

©Wendy O'Hanlon, December, 2021

Prejudice

Please Mister
Help me please
Tell me why
They all laugh at me.

Tell me why
As I go by
They watch me
With cruel laughing eyes.

Please Mister
Help me please
Tell me what
Is wrong with me.

Tell me why
They are better than me
Tell me why
I am not the same.

Continued next page

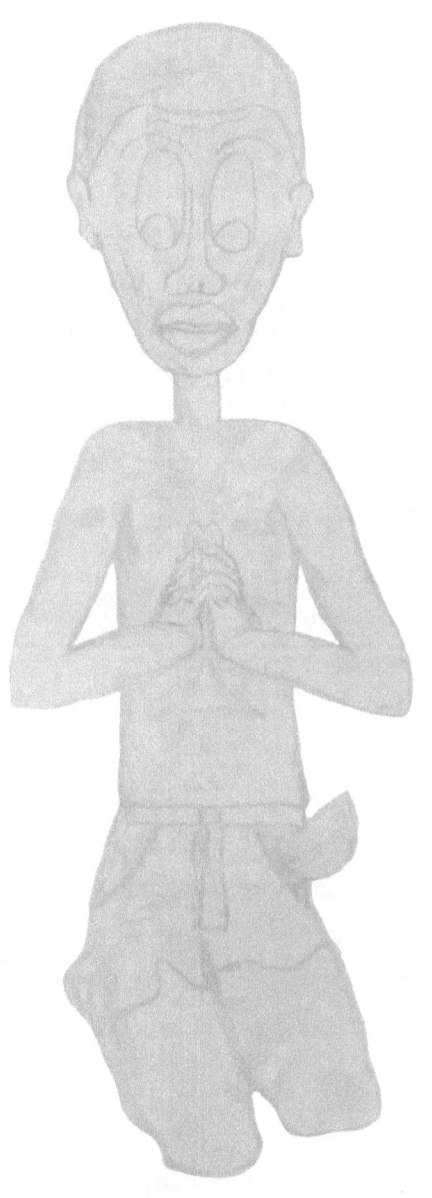

Please Mister
Tell me why
They throw stones at me
As I go by.

And laugh and call
To their mates
If my blood
Is painted on a stone.
Tell me Mister. Why?

Please Mister
Help me please
Don't go away!
Tell me why, Mister
Don't go away!
Please!
Mister!
Please!

©Wendy O'Hanlon, 1975

Written for a major Year 10 English project.

Illustration ©Wendy O'Hanlon, 1975

Viva La Revolution!

They treat us with contempt
We're just 'Facebook Warriors'
They snigger.

They vote behind closed doors
To monetise our Town Plan
Signing with a pen
To pull the trigger
At our age-old
Environment and wildlife.

Viva La Revolution!
Vote them out!
You work for us
Without a doubt.
But this you forgot
When you donned the 'big boy' pants.
And thought you knew better
Than the collective wisdom
Of your voters
Who put you there
In your expensive chair
In the first place.

Continued next page

Viva La Revolution!
We are not protesters
We are protectors
And we have galvanised
In to a force
To be reckoned with.
We wield the pen, we place the posters
We lobby ceaselessly
To remove you – once and for all.

We are knocking on your castle walls
Breaking down your
Closed–meeting doors
Uncovering your mates' deals.

Do not underestimate us,
Do not snigger
We will never give up
We have far more to lose
Than your engorged egos and pay packets.
We have eons, generations of evolution
To protect for the future.
A future where your legacy will be
Just a small dot in history.
Viva La Revolution!

©Wendy O'Hanlon, November 1, 2018

Wendy O'Hanlon

Wendy O'Hanlon grew up on a sugar-cane farm overlooking the Maroochy River and Mt Ninderry on the Sunshine Coast in Queensland.

Wendy wrote her first poem when she was six, according to family folklore, about her little brother Daren – "Daren the little Baron", and was first published in The Sunday-Mail at the age of 12 with her poem titled "A House - The Eremite" which was published later that year in the Queensland Schools Magazine. She wrote her first song at 13 when she was given a guitar as a birthday present.

Wendy is a poet and spoken-word performer, writer, journalist, editor, author, thespian, photographer, project traveller, artist, broadcaster, festival founder, workshop host, MC, voiceover specialist, singer-songwriter and, above all, the Mum of two amazing young men.

Her 30-plus-year career as a journalist took her to London's Fleet Street newspapers in the late '80s. She has worked for Asia-Pacific region publications and spent many years as a journalist and editor on the Sunshine Coast and in Brisbane. In 2016, Wendy founded the Sunshine Coast International Readers and Writers Festival, bringing writers and musicians from Australia, Indonesia and Europe to Coolum. In 2017, she founded the Sunshine Coast Poetry Slam Championships, the Sunshine Coast region becoming a part of the Queensland

Poetry Festival and Australian Poetry Slam Championships for the first time *ever,* and in 2018 started the fortnightly *Words@play* open-mic poetry nights at Foxy On Coolum.

As for broadcasting, in the late '80s Wendy spent an exciting year doing a special AIR-TV course founded by Radio 4BC (John Knox) and Channel 9 (Jim Iliffe) – and became their 1987 AIR-TV Dux. In 2019, she graduated from a radio broadcasting course and started hosting her own community radio show for three years. In 2022, she launched her own podcast – "P.O. Box 45 with Wendyoh" – which is available on Spotify, Youtube, Apple, Audible and Buzzsprout. Wendy's journey as an author, of what will be many books, has just begun.

www.girlwithwords.com

Illustrator Michelle Mann

Michelle Mann is a mixed media artist and illustrator living on the beautiful Sunshine Coast in Queensland, Australia. The Sunny Coast has been Michelle's home all her life, and although she has travelled to many destinations throughout the world, she still loves to come home to such paradise.

Michelle's current body of work is inspired by her connection with spirit and conveying that which is invisible into form. As well as larger works in acrylic and oil, Michelle also loves to illustrate for children's books, pattern design and creates travel journals. Michelle's work is vibrant, joyful and whimsical.

One of Michelle's biggest projects was creating the Gold Lotus Oracle deck where she painted all 47 images for the deck and wrote a book that accompanies the deck. The Gold Lotus Oracle deck is used for guidance and self-growth. It is a culmination of experience from her many years as a psychic medium and teacher.

Michelle has held two solo exhibitions, has won a number of awards for her Gold Lotus Oracle deck creation, was a finalist in the prestigious Houston Quilt show and her work has been displayed in galleries throughout South-East Queensland and in Sydney.

Her work is held by collectors both nationally and internationally. Most days you will find Michelle playing with colour in her home studio in Woombye.

www.michellemannart.com

...and a lot salty

Hi... from girlwithwords

Thank you all for buying, reading or flicking through my first poetry collection.

Words become poems, become lyrics, become songs, become theatre scripts and become movies. Words are our bedrock in communication.

Poetry books and spoken-word (performance poetry and slam poetry) encourage people of all ages to engage and emote - to express their feelings.

There is no right or wrong way to write poetry, performance poetry, music....

Just do it.

Find an open-mic group and share your words. The first time will be a bit scary but keep going. We poets are very supportive.

I would love you to share some of your poetry with me and be happy to share on my website *www.girlwithwords.com*.

Cheers,
Wendyoh.

Start your own poetry or spoken-word group/event

You know, it is really easy to get poets together – because we do crave that connection.

If you can't find a poetry group close to your area, then start one. Check out your nearest coffee shops or boutique café/bar venues and 'feel the vibe' – really! If you think that place could be a good venue for a poetry group, and you feel comfortable there… then chat to the owner or manager about organising something – a regular fortnightly event. (Once a week is too demanding, once a month is too disconnected… fortnightly is just right.) And your event gives the venue owner some regular patrons. Win, win!

If you are at high school, ask one of your English teachers to help you get this regular group going at school.

It is easy to start your own poetry/spoken-word event. I have done just that. And it was fun! We grew a family of more than 30 poets who will always stay connected.

And the story goes: "In 2017, we were looking for a comfy, laid-back venue in Coolum (Sunshine Coast, Queensland, Australia) to start a fortnightly poetry night with people reciting their poems and writings and generally just meeting, chatting and building up the courage to recite their works in public! And write more.

Being a writer, I came up with the event name: 'Words at play' - because we love playing with words, even making up new ones. Because we can - no spellchecks in poetry!

The rest is history. For three years *Words@play* was a very big fortnightly event at Ilana McBain's Foxy On Coolum café/bar. Poets, spoken-word performers, storytellers and singer-songwriters from across the Sunshine Coast had our event as a regular on their calendar."

In those three years, we watched poets of all ages find their voice. We welcomed so many new friends. We were all so different and we appreciated, encouraged and loved that difference.

The Pandemic Years... and creatives learned more about technology. We connected with poets and spoken-word performers across the world in so many social media groups, live-streamed backyard and verandah performances, videos... We learned so much about writing styles, cultures and stories.

So, now we can connect globally and face-to-face.

And, as I said, it is easy to start your own poetry spoken-word group. We had no idea what to expect when we started *Words@ play*. We are all amazingly happy that we did.

Cheers,
Wendyoh
Ends xxxxxxxxxxxx

Create your own poetry

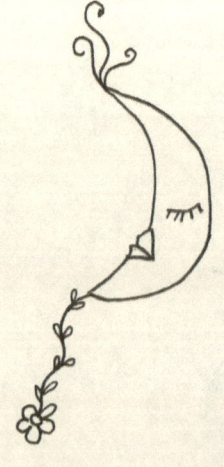

www.ingramcontent.com/pod-product-compliance
Lightning Source LLC
Chambersburg PA
CBHW030412120726
47904CB00007B/2247